Dora in Magic Land

Adapted by Mary Tillworth • Illustrated by Dan Haskett and Brenda Goddard
Based on the teleplay "Magic Land!" by Dustin Ferrer

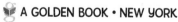 A GOLDEN BOOK • NEW YORK

T#: 424199

randomhousekids.com

ISBN 978-0-553-53840-3

Printed in the United States of America   10 9 8 7 6 5 4 3 2 1

Dora and Pablo were practicing magic tricks for a show they were about to perform in the twins' class. Pablo was trying to make a chain with his magic rings when Papi arrived with a special gift. It was his old magician's top hat!

Suddenly, a bunny popped out of the hat, jumped to the floor, and hopped away!

Dora and Pablo chased the bunny
into a magic shop . . .

up the stairs . . .

. . . and straight into a place called
Magic Land!
    Dora and Pablo caught up with
the bunny, but the top hat was gone.

A fortune-teller told them that a mean magician named Víctor had snatched the hat and was using it to steal all the magic tricks in Magic Land.

Map App told Dora to head north to find Víctor.

Dora and her friends found Víctor
in the Card Garden.

"I need Papi's hat back, *por favor*,"
Dora said.

"No—it's mine!" shouted Víctor.
By waving the magic hat, he conjured
up a cave and disappeared into it!

There was a pit in the cave. It was very deep.
Dora knew how they could get to the bottom.
"Abracadabra!" she called. A magic rope appeared
in her hand, and one end of it flew down into the pit.

Dora, Pablo, and the bunny climbed down the rope and ran through the cave. At the exit, they saw Víctor using the magic hat to make a tall cliff appear out of nowhere!

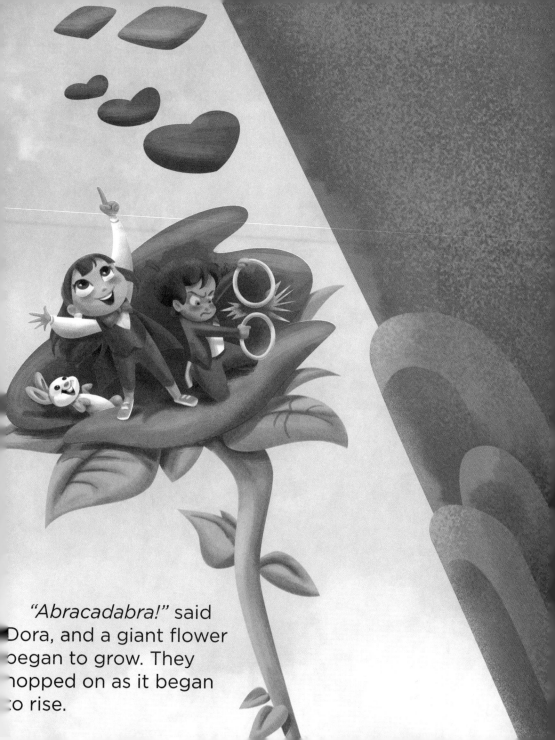

"*Abracadabra!*" said
Dora, and a giant flower
began to grow. They
hopped on as it began
to rise.

Víctor spotted Dora and her friends, and he waved the top hat again. This time, a magic carpet appeared. "You'll never catch me now!" he said, laughing as he flew off.

"*Abracadabra!*" called Dora, and a small balloon bird appeared!

"*¡Crece, globo!*" shouted the friends. The balloon bird grew until it was big enough for them to ride!

The friends chased Víctor across the sky. Then the mean magician waved the top hat and a magic storm spilled out!

But a gust of wind suddenly blew the hat away!

The hat landed on a storm cloud, just out of reach.

"Pablo! You can use your rings to get the hat back!" said Dora.

Taking a deep breath, Pablo clinked his rings together—and made a long chain. His trick had worked!

Dora twirled the chain over her head and lassoed the top hat. Then, with a wave of the hat, Dora made the storm disappear.

The friends landed safely on the ground,
and Dora used Papi's hat one more time.
"Return all the magic tricks to Magic Land!"
she said.

All the tricks flew out of the hat
and back to their owners!

"Dora and Pablo, you saved Magic Land!" cheered everyone.

Dora smiled. "And now we need to get back to our own magic show!" She and Pablo waved goodbye and zoomed home to Playa Verde.

Back in the twins' classroom, Dora and Pablo put on a wonderful show.

"Thanks for bringing magic to our school!" said the kids.

Dora smiled at Pablo. "We did it together!"